For my grand nieces: Talia Yiting Buckley and
Ada Yilin Buckley, both dear little ones.
—N. L.

For Charlie, constant wanderer of this wonderful world. Thank
you for 20 years of the most epic adventures and friendship!
You make this earth even more beautiful with you in it.
—M. C.

SIMON & SCHUSTER BOOKS FOR YOUNG READERS • An imprint of Simon & Schuster Children's Publishing Division 1230 Avenue of the Americas, New York, New York 10020 • Text © 2021 by Nina Laden • Illustration © 2021 by Melissa Castrillón Book design by Lizzy Bromley © 2021 by Simon & Schuster, Inc. • All rights reserved, including the right of reproduction in whole or in part in any form. • SIMON & SCHUSTER BOOKS FOR YOUNG READERS and related marks are trademarks of Simon & Schuster, Inc. • For information about special discounts for bulk purchases, please contact • Simon & Schuster Special Sales at 1-866-506-1949 or business@simonandschuster.com. • The Simon & Schuster Speakers Bureau can bring authors to your live event. • For more information or to book an event, contact the Simon & Schuster Speakers Bureau at 1-866-248-3049 or visit our website at www.simonspeakers.com. The text for this book was set in Simoncini Garamond. • The illustrations for this book were rendered in in pencil and then colored digitally. • Manufactured in China • 0821 SCP • First Edition • 2 4 6 8 10 9 7 5 3 1 • Library of Congress Cataloging-in-Publication Data • Names: Laden, Nina, author. | Castrillon, Melissa, illustrator. • Title: Dear Little One / Nina Laden ; illustrated by Melissa Castrillon. • Description: First edition. | New York : Simon & Schuster Books for Young Readers, [2021] | "A Paula Wiseman book." | Audience: Ages 4-8. | Audience: Grades K-1. | Summary: "This lyrical picture book celebrates all the wonder and beauty in the natural world, featuring Mother Nature personified. From the treasure of flowers to the mystery of insects this book encourages children to explore their world and be grateful for all that surrounds them"—Provided by publisher. • Identifiers: LCCN 2021000035 (print) | LCCN 2021000036 (eBook) | • ISBN 9781534454774 (hardcover) | ISBN 9781534454781 (eBook) • Subjects: CYAC: Stories in rhyme. | Nature—Fiction. • Classification: LCC PZ8.3.L125 De 2021 (print) | LCC PZ8.3.L125 (eBook) | DDC [E]—dc23 • LC record available at https://lccn.loc.gov/2021000035 • LC ebook record available at https://lccn.loc.gov/2021000036

Dear Little One

Nina Laden
Melissa Castrillon

A Paula Wiseman Book
Simon & Schuster Books for Young Readers
New York London Toronto Sydney New Delhi

Dear Little One

Your time on
Earth has just
begun.

Take in the sights.
Take in the sound.
Take in the scents
that excite and astound.

Celebrate the flowers.
Be grateful for bees.

Their work bears fruit.
Worship the trees.

Investigate insects,
some glow and shine.

Inspect spiderwebs
and their lovely design.

Watch plants grow.
Start them from seeds.

Be enchanted by ferns.
Examine the weeds.

Dig in the ground.
Find worms and stones.
Look for ancient fossils
or long-buried bones.

Hike in the forests.
They make the world green.
Their leaves act like lungs
to keep the air clean.

Love mammals and birds,
reptiles and amphibians too,
in their natural habitat,
not just in a zoo.

Visit oceans and lakes
faraway and near.

Swim with
the fish
in water
so clear.

Treasure the deserts.
Explore the sand.

Climb up the mountains.
Be good to the land.

Be thankful for the wind,

the rain,

and the snow.

Be in awe of the sun
that makes everything grow.

Marvel at the stars,
and the vastness of space.
You are a sparkling part
of this beautiful place.

Care for this world.
It will be a friend to you,
and be there for your children,
and their children too.

Bring peace to our Earth.
Help keep it from danger.

I send you my blessings.
Love, Mother Nature